HELP!

I'M TRAPPED IN
OBEDIENCE SCHOOL AGAIN

HELP!
I'M TRAPPED IN OBEDIENCE SCHOOL AGAIN

TODD STRASSER

AN
APPLE
PAPERBACK

SCHOLASTIC INC.
New York   Toronto   London   Auckland   Sydney

No part of this publication may be reproduced in whole or in part, or stored in a retrieval system, or transmitted in any form or by any means, electronic, mechanical, photocopying, recording, or otherwise, without written permission of the publisher. For information regarding permission, write to Scholastic Inc., 555 Broadway, New York, NY 10012.

ISBN 0-590-02971-1

12 11 10 9 8 7 6 5 4 3 2   7 8 9/9 0 1 2/0

Printed in the U.S.A.   40

First Scholastic printing, September 1997

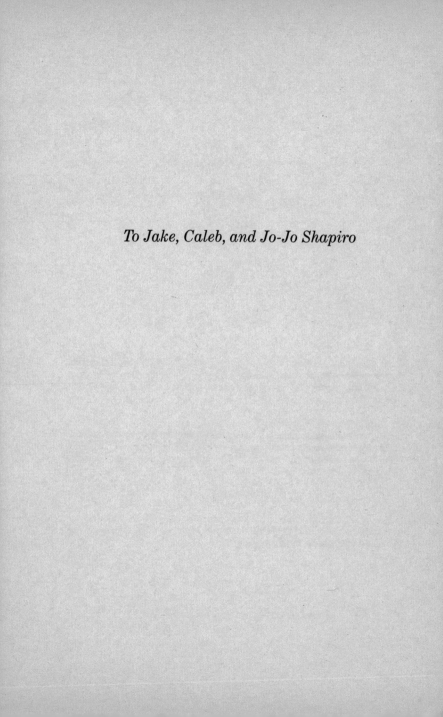

To Jake, Caleb, and Jo-Jo Shapiro

HELP!
I'M TRAPPED IN
OBEDIENCE SCHOOL AGAIN

1

"Come on, Andy," I said. "All I need is the nose and I'll have the whole face in The Holey Donut Face Puzzle Contest. That'll qualify me for the super home entertainment center."

My friend Andy Kent yawned. He, Josh Hopka, and I were sitting on the curb outside The Holey Donut, eating donuts for breakfast. It was Saturday morning: no school.

"Forget about the contest," Josh said. "Listen, Andy, if you give me the fifth issue of Mole Man Comix, I'll have a complete set. I can sell it at the comic book show in a few weeks and make a fortune."

"Watch this," Andy said. He bit off the corner of his Holey Donut napkin and chewed it. Then he rolled the soggy, chewed part into a big fat spitball and stuck it into one of his nostrils.

Then he tilted his head back.

Then he pressed his other nostril shut with his finger.

1

Snort! The spitball shot out of his nose and across the parking lot. *Splat!* It landed on the windshield of a parked car.

Josh and I were speechless.

"Cool, huh?" Andy grinned.

Josh made a face. "That was completely gross."

"Bet you couldn't do it," Andy said.

"Bet I *wouldn't want* to do it," Josh shot back. "Anyone ever tell you that you're totally sick, Andy?"

"Don't make him mad," I said. "We both need stuff from him."

"Forget it," Andy said. "Jake, I'm not giving you the nose. And Josh, I'm *definitely* not giving you the fifth issue of Mole Man."

"Wait, Andy," I said. "I'll make a deal. You name it. There has to be *something* you'd want in return. Whatever it is, I'll get it for you."

Andy stared off across the street. Some cars went past, and people were out jogging and walking their dogs. "Okay, there is something I want. And if you can get it for me I'll give you the nose."

"Great," I said. "What is it?"

Andy pointed. "*Her.*"

2

Josh and I looked across the street. A girl with short brown hair and a turned-up nose was walking a small dog. The dog also had short brown hair and a turned-up nose.

"Who is she?" I asked.

"Her name is Mica Channing," Andy said. "She's new in town."

"So?" said Josh.

"I like her," Andy said.

"Do you know her?" I asked.

Andy shook his head.

"Then how do you know you like her?" Josh asked.

"I just do," said Andy.

"Then go talk to her," I said.

Andy shook his head.

"Why not?" I asked.

Andy shrugged and gazed down at the ground.

Josh smiled. "Don't you get it, Jake? Andy's too shy."

"Drop dead." Andy shoved him.

"Why don't you blow a big juicy spitball out your nose at her?" Josh asked. "I bet she'd really like that."

"Bug off," Andy grumbled.

But Josh was on his case now. "I really don't get you, Andy. Don't you know she's a *girl*. How can you like her?"

"Why not?" Andy asked.

"Because guys our age aren't supposed to be interested in girls," Josh said. "We only like sports, video games, and pizza."

"Some guys our age like girls," Andy said.

"Sure," said Josh. "And some guys our age play with dolls."

"Give him a break," I said. "Just because he likes a girl doesn't mean he wants to play with dolls."

"Well, if he likes her, he should go meet her," Josh said.

"No," Andy said.

"Why not?" asked Josh.

"Because it's not that easy," I answered for Andy. "Right now she doesn't know him. If he just walks up and starts talking to her, she might think he's weird or too pushy. It has to be a *natural* meeting."

Josh stared at me. "How do *you* know?"

"Because of my sister," I said.

"Jessica?" Josh said.

4

"Does Jake have any *other* sisters?" Andy asked with a smirk.

"She always complains about how hard it is to meet nice guys," I said. "She says the ones who are bold enough to walk up and introduce themselves are usually jerks. The nice ones are too shy. So she never gets to meet them."

"That's not the reason Jessica can't meet guys," Josh said. "The real reason is that she shaved off her hair."

"She didn't *shave* it," I said. "She just had it cut really short."

"Same difference," Josh said with a shrug. "Now she's so ugly the shower drain has nicer hair. *That's* why she can't meet guys."

Across the street, a white-haired old guy walked a small white dog toward Mica and her dog. The two dogs stopped and sniffed each other. Mica and the old guy started to chat.

Andy straightened up and smiled. "I think I just got an idea."

3

"I'm not sure I understand this," Josh said later. He, Andy, and I were walking up the street toward my house. "You want to walk Jake's dog, Lance, so you can meet Mica?"

"You got it." Andy nodded. "She walks her dog every afternoon after school. She takes it everywhere she goes."

We turned up my driveway. I took out my key and opened the front door.

"Bad garbage can!" someone shouted from the kitchen. "Bad, bad garbage can!"

Josh and Andy both gave me strange looks.

"I guess Jessica's home," I said.

We went into the kitchen. The floor was covered with torn food wrappers, coffee grounds, orange peels, and other garbage.

Lance, our eighty-pound Labrador retriever, was cowering in the corner. His ears and tail were down, as if he knew he'd done something wrong.

Jessica was standing by the sink with her

hands on her hips. Her hair was cut so short you could see her scalp. Half a dozen earrings dangled from each ear, and her fingernails were painted black. She glared down at the overturned garbage can on the floor and yelled, "Bad, bad garbage can!"

"Ahem!" I cleared my throat.

My sister looked up. "Oh, hi, guys." Then she looked back down at the garbage can. "Bad garbage can! Very bad garbage can!"

Josh, Andy, and I shared an uncomfortable glance.

"If I were you, I'd be a little worried, Jake," Josh whispered.

The truth was, I *was* a little worried. Why in the world was Jessica yelling at the garbage can? I figured I'd take the calm approach. "So, uh, it looks like Lance got into the garbage again."

"That's very observant of you, Jake," my sister said. She picked up the large white plastic garbage can and shook it. "Bad, bad garbage can!"

"Just out of curiosity," I said. "Why are you yelling at the garbage can?"

Jessica pointed at the floor. "Look at this mess."

"Then shouldn't you be yelling at *Lance*?" I asked.

"Let me ask you a question, Jake." Jessica crossed her arms. "How many times has Lance

7

gotten into the kitchen garbage this month?"

"About ten times," I said.

"And how many times have I yelled at him?" Jessica asked.

"About ten times," I said again.

"And has that stopped him?" she asked.

"No," I said. "But what makes you think yelling at the garbage can will stop him?"

"This." My sister picked up an orange and black book called *The Total Idiot's Guide to Dog Training*.

"They sure named it for the right person," Josh quipped.

Jessica glared at him. "Very funny, Josh."

"It says you should yell at garbage cans?" I asked.

Jessica nodded. "Lance has feelings just like we do. When he gets into the garbage, he doesn't know he's going to make a mess. So you're supposed to yell at the garbage can. That way the dog gets the idea that he's done something wrong, but you don't have to hurt his feelings."

"I think you'd be better off sending him back to obedience school," Josh said.

"I don't have the time to take him to obedience school again," my sister said. "And I don't want to spend the money. But if this doesn't work, I'm going to have to. Because Dad says if Lance doesn't stop getting into the garbage we're going to have to get rid of him."

A tear actually appeared in Jessica's eye. She wiped it away and got down on her knees beside Lance, who was now lying on the kitchen floor, fast asleep. The older Lance got, the more he slept. Jessica gathered his big, furry head in her arms and hugged him.

"There's no way I'm ever going to let my big love puppy go away," she sniffed.

Josh, Andy, and I watched my nearly bald sister hug and kiss our dog. Lance opened his eyes and started to lick her face. At moments like that, I was certain Jessica was a mental case.

4

"Listen, Jessica," I said. "If you really want Lance to stop raiding the garbage can, maybe you should feed him something *good* once in a while."

"What are you talking about?" My sister stood up and pointed at a big blue dog-food can in the corner. "I feed him *Canine Connoisseur*. It's the best dog food money can buy."

"It may be the best," I said, "but it's still dog food." I went over to the can and pulled off the top. I pointed at the round, brown *Canine Connoisseur* pellets inside. "Look at that stuff. Take a whiff of it. It *stinks*! If I was a dog, I'd definitely eat garbage before I ate *that*."

"But you're not a dog," my sister said.

"I wouldn't be so sure," Josh said with a grin.

"You're a laugh and a half," I mumbled at him.

"*Canine Connoisseur* is formulated to give Lance the exact balance of proteins, vitamins, and carbohydrates he needs," Jessica said, sounding like a commercial. "And it's made with the highest quality chicken, beef, and fish by-products."

"Don't you know what by-products are?" I asked. "By-products are the parts we'd *never buy*! Like eyeballs and noses and brains."

"But Lance likes it," Jessica insisted.

"Get real," I said. "If you gave him a choice between *Canine Connoisseur* and a nice, juicy hamburger, which do you think he'd eat?"

"Well . . ." Jessica hesitated.

I crossed my arms and smiled. "I rest my case."

My sister sighed. "Would you guys mind telling me what you're doing here? I mean, is there something you want or do you just enjoy giving me grief?"

Andy nudged me with his elbow. Jessica saw him do it. She smiled smugly. "Okay, I know you want something. What is it?"

Andy nudged me again. I cleared my throat. "Well, uh, you know how you're always complaining that no one takes care of Lance except you? Like no one else feeds him or brushes him or walks him? How would you like some help?"

The wrinkles in Jessica's forehead deepened. "What kind of help?"

"How would you like Andy to walk Lance every day after school for you?" I asked.

My sister blinked with surprise, then frowned and shook her head. "Never."

"Why not?" I asked.

11

"Because I won't allow it," Jessica said.

"But *why*?"

"I don't have to give you a reason," she said. "But the answer is positively, definitely, absolutely no."

"But — " I started to say.

"Forget it, Jake," Andy said. "Let's drop it."

My friends and I left the kitchen.

"What a bummer," Josh moped. "If Jessica won't let Andy walk Lance, you can't get the nose for The Holey Donut Face Puzzle Contest and I can't get the fifth issue of Mole Man."

"I'm not giving up," I said. "I'll wait until later and talk to her again."

5

That night after dinner I knocked on Jessica's door and went into her room. I knew my sister would be in a good mood because she was going out with some friends, and she was hoping to meet some guy named Kirk who she liked. Jessica was sitting at her makeup table, putting dark eyeliner around her eyes.

"What do you want?" she asked when she saw me in her mirror.

I wanted to talk about Andy and Lance, but seeing her with those dark rings around her eyes distracted me.

"Jess, I hate to say this," I said, "but do you really think this guy Kirk is going to be attracted to you?"

"Why not?" Jessica said, still looking in the mirror.

"Don't you think having black eyes and fingernails, and no hair, and a thousand earrings makes you look a little weird?" I asked.

13

"No," my sister replied. "But even if it did, what's *wrong* with being a little different?"

"It's not *different*," I said. "It's *weird*."

"You want to know what's weird?" Jessica asked. "*You* are, Jake. You're so normal you're weird."

"I am not," I said.

"Are too," said my sister.

"Listen," I said, "I can be just as weird as you."

"No way."

"Oh, yeah? Watch." I took a tissue from the box on her makeup table, bit off a corner, and chewed it up. When I had a nice, juicy spitball, I stuck it in my nose. Tilting my head back, and holding the other nostril shut, I shot the spitball across the room.

Splat! It hit Jessica's door.

"See?" I said.

"That's not weird," Jessica said. "That's absolutely, totally gross."

"Then how about this?" I opened Jessica's door. Pressing my hands and feet against the insides of the doorway, I inched my way up to the top.

"Sorry." Jessica shook her head. "That's not weird, either. That's just showing off. Face it, Jake. You're too normal. You'll never be able to be weird."

"That's totally not true," I said as I climbed back down. "I can be as weird as you. I just have to think of something."

"Well, why don't you go think in *your* room and leave me alone, okay?" Jessica suggested.

"I will, but first I need to talk to you about Andy and Lance," I said, sitting down on the corner of her bed.

Jessica put down her eyeliner and turned to me. "Forget it. There's no way I'm going to let him walk my dog."

"Why not?" I asked. "You're always complaining that no one helps you with Lance. This is the perfect opportunity."

"No." Jessica shook her nearly bald head.

"Why?"

"Because it's a trick," she said. "Andy doesn't really want to walk Lance. He just wants to use Lance to get something."

"How do you know that?" I asked.

"Because I know you and your friends, Jake," my sister said. "Admit it."

I took a deep breath and let it out slowly. "Okay, Jess, you're right. Andy *does* want to use Lance for something."

Jessica looked surprised. "You actually *admit* it?"

"Yes," I said. Then I explained the whole story of Mica Channing, and how Andy wanted to meet her.

Jessica looked shocked. "That's . . . that's so sweet."

"So you see why Andy wants to walk Lance," I

said. "And I promise he'll take good care of him."

Jessica thought it over, then nodded. "All right, but I want him to promise, too. I want him to *swear* he'll take good care of my love puppy. If anything ever happens to Lance . . . if you or your friends ever do anything to him. And I mean, *anything* . . . I'd never forgive you. Understand?"

"Yes." I nodded solemnly. But inside I wanted to shout for joy. Now that Jessica had agreed to let Andy walk Lance, I was one step closer to entering The Holey Donut Face Puzzle Contest, and winning the super home entertainment center.

6

For the next two weeks, Andy walked Lance every day. In the meantime, I tried to prove to Jessica that I could be just as weird as her. Not that I cut off all my hair or wore makeup, but I did do some pretty weird stuff.

I put my plate on the floor and ate dinner like a dog.

I wore one of my father's ties around my head like a headband.

I wore two different socks and two different shoes to school.

I walked around backward.

Jessica said I was trying too hard. She said I had to be *naturally* weird.

While I was trying too hard to be weird, Andy was trying to meet Mica.

On Thursday morning we sat together on the curb outside The Holey Donut. We had no school that day because of a teachers' conference.

"So how's it going?" I asked him.

"Not good," Andy moped. "I'm paying a lot of attention to Lance, but Mica's not paying any attention to me."

"What's the problem?" I asked.

"Lance," Andy said. "Every time I see Mica with her dog, I try to get Lance to walk toward them. But Lance could care less. All he wants to do is chase squirrels. I've seen Mica every day after school this week. But every time I see her, Lance pulls me in the wrong direction."

I nodded sympathetically. Lance was a big dog, and when he wanted to go somewhere nothing stopped him. I felt bad for Andy, but I had problems of my own. The deadline for The Holey Donut Face Puzzle Contest was that night.

"Listen, Andy," I said. "I have to have a complete puzzle in the mail by midnight or I won't qualify for a chance to win the home entertainment center. All I need is the nose."

Instead of answering, Andy bit off the corner of his napkin and started to chew it.

"Come on, Andy," I said. "You can't use the nose. After tonight it will be totally useless. At least let me have a chance."

Andy made a big, juicy spitball and stuck it in his nose. He still wouldn't answer me. I was starting to feel really frustrated.

"I really don't get you," I said. "Why won't you give it to me? You can't be that selfish. What do you want?"

Andy tilted his head back. *Snort!* He shot the spitball out of his nose at a passing car.

Splat! The spitball hit the car door.

"I want to make a deal," he said.

"Let me guess," I said. "You want some of my video games?"

Andy shook his head.

"My Mega-Soaker Machine Water Gun?"

"Nope," said Andy.

"My Rollerblades?"

"Nope."

"Then what?" I asked.

"I want you to switch bodies with Lance," Andy said.

7

It wasn't as far-fetched as it sounded. Our science teacher, Mr. Dirksen, had built a machine that was supposed to transfer intelligence from one person to another. But all it really did was make you switch bodies. I'd already switched bodies with Mr. Dirksen; Mr. Braun, my gym teacher; the President of the United States; and Jessica.

Still, it wasn't something you did every day. I stared at him like he was out of his mind. "Are you crazy?"

"Look," Andy said. "You asked me what I wanted in return for the nose and I told you."

"But why?"

"Because with you in Lance's body, I'll get to meet Mica," Andy explained. "I won't have to worry about you dragging me away to chase squirrels."

"But I can't switch bodies with Lance," I said. "I have to go to school tomorrow."

"It'll just be for today," Andy said. "The teachers are all at that conference. We could sneak in this morning and make the switch. Then we'll go back this afternoon and make the switch back."

"But what if something goes wrong?" I asked. "What if I get stuck in Lance's body longer than that?"

"It's not so bad," Andy said. "Remember what happened to me? I was stuck in Lance's body for a couple of days. Lance went to school in my body and did fine."

"Except that we all got sent to Principal Blanco's office because you barked in Mr. Dirksen's science class," I reminded him.

"But we didn't get into any *real* trouble," Andy said. He bit off another piece of napkin while I thought it over. Switching bodies with Lance sounded risky, but as I said before, I'd already switched bodies with several people. In each case I'd been able to switch back without harm. In addition, Andy had switched with Lance, and once, for a moment, Principal Blanco had switched with a toad. Everyone had been able to switch back without a problem.

"Just think," Andy said. "You'll have the nose piece, which will complete the entire face puzzle, and make you eligible to win that huge home entertainment center. You'll be the most popular kid in the whole school!"

It was tempting.

"There's just one problem," I said. "If I switch bodies with Lance, that means Lance has to switch bodies with me. Who's going to watch Lance in my body to make sure he doesn't get into trouble while I'm in his body?"

Andy pointed down the sidewalk.

Josh was walking toward us.

8

A moment later Josh sat down on the curb with us.

"Listen, Andy," he said. "The comic-book show is tonight. You *have* to let me have the fifth issue of Mole Man. With the whole collection of Mole Man Comix I can make a fortune."

"Okay." Andy nodded.

"I mean, I really don't see why you won't give it to me," Josh went on. "What good is one issue to you? You probably haven't even looked at it in years."

"You're right," Andy said. "It's all yours."

"And the thing is," Josh went on, "you're my friend. Friends are supposed to help each other. And you — " Josh suddenly stopped. "What did you just say?"

"I said you can have the fifth issue of Mole Man Comix," Andy said.

Josh looked over at me. "Is he feeling okay?"

"I think there's more to it," I said.

"Ah ha!" Josh nodded. "There's a catch! I should have known. Andy will give me the comic, but in return I have to mow his lawn next summer. Or I have to do his homework for him. Or paint his house. Right? It's going to be something ridiculous. Something impossible."

"You have to watch Jake today," Andy said.

Josh blinked. "What?"

"Watch me," I said.

"Why can't you watch yourself?" Josh asked.

"Because he's not going to be himself," Andy explained. "He's going to be Lance."

Josh buried his face in his hands. "Oh, no, not again!"

9

"It won't be so bad," Andy said a few moments later as we walked back to my house to get Lance.

"That's easy for *you* to say," Josh scoffed.

"Was it so bad when Lance was in my body?" Andy asked.

"Oh, nooooo, you were really easy." Josh rolled his eyes. "Except you chewed up the leg of my mom's table, then had to be walked, then barked at a policeman and almost got me arrested, then climbed into a tree and couldn't get down. You were a piece of cake, Andy."

"Well, that's the only deal I'm willing to make," Andy said. "Take it or leave it."

"Yeah, right," Josh muttered. "Only if I don't take it I'll probably wind up watching Lance in Jake's body all day anyway. So why not get something out of it?"

"Smart boy." Andy grinned.

We got to my house and went inside. Since it was Thursday, both of my parents had gone to work.

"Jessica, you here?" I called out.

"In the kitchen," she called back.

We went into the kitchen. It was a mess. Garbage was spread all over the floor. Jessica was sweeping it up.

"Did Lance get into the garbage again?" Josh asked.

"No, I did," my sister replied, obviously in a bad mood. "I just love getting up in the morning and rummaging through the garbage for table scraps."

Josh nodded. "I always thought you were strange."

Jessica smirked.

"If Dad finds out, he's gonna be really ticked," I said. "This might be the straw that breaks the camel's back."

"Well, Dad's *not* going to find out, okay?" Jessica said.

"I bet you won't mind if I take Lance for a walk," Andy said. He looked around. "Where is he anyway?"

"Where else?" Jessica pointed at a sunny spot in the corner of the kitchen. Lance was asleep on his back with his legs in the air and his tongue hanging out of the corner of his mouth.

"Why don't you take him for a nice, *long* walk and give me time to clean up," Jessica said. "And after that, I'm going to see when obedience school begins."

"My pleasure," Andy replied with a smile.

10

A few minutes later we headed toward school. Every time Lance smelled something that interested him, he'd start to pull Andy in that direction.

"Can't you control him?" Josh asked.

"Get real," Andy grunted as Lance pulled him toward a tree. "This dog weighs almost as much as I do and he can use *four* legs instead of two." He turned to me. "Why can't we let him off the leash, Jake? Then I won't have to follow him everywhere."

"Because there's a new leash law in town," I explained. "If they catch your dog running free, you get a ticket and the dog can be sent to the animal shelter."

"I still don't understand how we're going to get Lance into school," Josh said. "We're not even supposed to be in school today. And dogs are *never* supposed to be there."

"Where there's a will, there's a way," Andy replied, making a right turn.

"Wait a minute," I said. "This isn't the way to school."

"You're right," Andy replied. "It's the way *to* the way to school."

"What're you talking about?" Josh asked.

"You'll see," said Andy.

We went to Andy's house. It turned out that his next door neighbor, Mr. Dunstable, owned the private custodial company that cleaned Burt Itchupt Middle School and the other schools in the district. Sneaking into Mr. Dunstable's garage, we "borrowed" some old, dark green Dunstable Cleaning and Maintenance Company coveralls. We also found a big fifty-five-gallon drum on wheels, and managed to get Lance into it.

"You can't seriously believe that Principal Blanco's going to fall for this," Josh moaned a little while later as we walked toward school wearing the coveralls and carrying brooms.

"Why not?" Andy asked. "Isn't he always telling us that if our grades don't improve we'll probably end up being janitors?"

I had to laugh. He had a good point.

We walked up to the school entrance, and Josh

pushed open the doors. Inside we were greeted by a large blue banner with white letters:

Welcome to Educational Networking Day
Dedicated to Doing More
for Our Students' Futures
Sponsored by the State Commission
on Excellence in Education

With Andy pushing the fifty-five-gallon drum with Lance inside, we passed the banner and went in. The halls were empty.

"This could be easier than I thought," Andy whispered as we started down the hall that led to Mr. Dirksen's lab.

The doors to the school auditorium were closed. Inside, we could hear the sound of a crowd.

"That must be where they're networking," I whispered.

As we passed the second set of doors, one of them swung open. Out came Principal Blanco, dressed in a dark suit. He was talking to a tall, red-headed woman wearing a green dress and carrying a black leather briefcase.

"Hello, boys," he said with a nod as we passed.

Josh, Andy, and I nodded back, and continued down the hall. We shared furtive looks. Was it possible that we'd actually fooled him?

"Hey, wait a minute!" a voice called behind us. "Where do you think you're going?"

11

Andy, Josh, and I froze, then slowly turned around. Principal Blanco and the red-headed woman were coming toward us.

"Where are you three going?" the principal asked with a frown. "What are you doing in those clothes?"

"We're working, Mr. Blanco," Andy replied.

"You work for Dunstable Cleaning and Maintenance?" Principal Blanco asked with a scowl.

"Yes, sir." Andy nodded.

"They look awfully young to be employed," said the red-headed woman.

"Uh, yes, well, they're students here," Mr. Blanco said.

"Hello, boys." The red-haired woman extended her hand and we shook it. "I'm Katherine Stuart, head of the Governor's Commission on Excellence in Education. Do you really do maintenance work?"

"It's a custodian training program," said Andy. "We do it on our days off."

Katherine Stuart rubbed her chin thoughtfully. "Forgive me for saying this, boys, but you're still young. There are fantastic opportunities in fields like communications and computer science. Don't you think you're selling yourselves short by training to be custodians?"

"But Principal Blanco always tells us this is all we'll ever be good for," Andy replied.

Katherine Stuart gave Principal Blanco a pensive look. The principal swallowed nervously. "Well I . . . I . . . *might* have said that as a joke," he sputtered. "But I never expected them to take me at my word."

"But you're our *principal*, sir," Josh said. "You're our leader and highest authority figure. We *always* take you at your word."

"Honestly, Mr. Blanco," Ms. Stuart said, "how on earth do you expect students to realize their fullest potentials if you don't encourage them?"

"Well, er, as I said, I might have said that, but I wasn't really *serious*," Principal Blanco stammered nervously. Meanwhile, Katherine Stuart took a pad and pen from her briefcase and started writing something. That seemed to make Principal Blanco even more nervous.

"Please understand, Ms. Stuart, we do a lot of kidding around in this school," he tried to explain. "I mean, you can't seriously believe that I'd encourage three of our brightest students to do maintenance work. . . ."

Andy nudged me with his elbow and nodded down the hall toward the science lab. Mr. Blanco was so busy trying to explain himself to Ms. Stuart, he didn't even notice when we left.

12

We got to Mr. Dirksen's lab and shut the door behind us.

"Phew, that was close," Andy groaned.

"Yeah," I agreed. "Good thing Ms. Stuart from the Governor's Commission on Excellence in Education was there."

"I bet from now on Principal Blanco only encourages us to be neurosurgeons," quipped Josh.

Groof! Groof! From inside the fifty-five-gallon drum came the sound of scratching and barking.

"Sounds like Lance wants to get out of that can," I said.

Andy opened the top of the drum and Lance bounded out. Wagging his tail like crazy, he started sniffing around the room.

"We better do this fast," Andy said. "Once Principal Blanco gets away from Ms. Stuart, he's probably going to come looking for us."

"Just don't forget," Josh said as he got behind the computer console attached to the Dirksen Intelligence Transfer System. "When this is over, you owe me the fifth issue of Mole Man."

"And I get the nose piece," I said as I got into one of the reclining chairs.

"You got it," Andy said. He turned to Lance. "Here, boy."

Lance gave Andy a curious look. Andy reached into the pocket of his coveralls and took out a dog biscuit. When Lance saw it, his mouth parted into a grin.

"Here you go, Lance," Andy said, holding the biscuit over the second reclining chair. Lance eagerly jumped into the chair.

"Now!" Andy cried.

Josh pushed a red button on the computer.

Whump!

Everything went black.

13

The first thing I noticed when I woke up was that I had something in my mouth. I bit into it and it crumbled. It tasted sort of bland and a little sweet, like a stale cookie. But I felt hungry and ate it anyway.

Then I noticed that Andy was staring at me with an amazed expression on his face.

"Jake?" he said.

"Urguh." I tried to answer but I couldn't speak. Instead, a tangle of sounds came out of my mouth. And the chair I was in felt awfully uncomfortable. I decided to get down.

The next thing I knew, I was on all four feet. Around me was a sea of chair and table legs. I looked down at my feet. But they weren't feet anymore. They were paws.

Ruff!

I heard a bark and looked around.

Suddenly, I was face to face with . . . me!

Well, it was Lance in my body, actually.

Grrrrrrr! Lance was on my hands and knees. He bared my teeth and growled at me.

Ruff! Ruff! Lance in my body barked again.

He looked really mad.

Lance was normally a really friendly dog.

He only had one problem. He didn't like other big, male dogs.

Sometimes he even attacked them.

And I looked exactly like a big, male dog to him.

Ruff! Lance in my body sprang at me!

14

"Whoa there, Jake." Andy grabbed Lance in my body, by the collar of my coveralls and held him back. Lance in my body was still on his hands and knees. Josh and Andy stood over us, looking down.

"Can you believe this?" Josh asked.

"No," Andy replied. "Every time it happens it's totally bizarre to me."

"*Urguh.*" I tried to tell them that it wasn't so bad, but I couldn't get Lance's mouth to make the words.

"I think he's trying to say something," Josh said.

"Forget it, Jake," Andy said. "When I was in Lance's body I couldn't talk either."

Ruff! Ruff! But Lance in my body could definitely bark. Andy was still holding him by the collar.

"Okay, listen," Andy said. "We better get out of here before Principal Blanco comes looking for us." He looked down at me. "Jake, you have to get back in the barrel."

Arf! I barked a yes.

Andy turned to Josh. "We have to get Jake, I mean, Lance, to stand up and walk out of here like a human being."

Josh and Andy helped Lance in my body to his feet. They walked him around the science lab a couple of times so he could get used to standing. It might have almost looked normal except his mouth was open and his tongue was hanging out. And he kept sniffing everything.

"Okay, let's get out of here," Andy finally said. Leaving Lance in my body with Josh, he helped me, in Lance's body, into the fifty-five-gallon drum. "Stay cool, Jake," he said, then placed the lid on the drum. Inside it became pitch-dark.

With a slight lurch, Andy started to push the drum. Inside, I couldn't see anything, but I could feel us moving. Everything seemed to be going smoothly and I imagined us leaving the science lab and going down the hall.

Then I felt a sudden jolt as we stopped. The lid of the drum opened slightly, letting some light in.

"Emergency!" Andy hissed. "It's Ms. Governor's Commission."

The lid slid shut and I was in darkness again.

"You're finished already?" I heard Ms. Stuart ask.

"Yes, ma'am," answered Andy.

"I think it's very admirable that you boys have chosen to work on your day off," Ms. Stuart said. "I just want you to remember that there are many opportunities for employment in your futures. Don't feel that you have to settle on a career so soon."

Ruff! I heard a bark. It must've been Lance in my body.

"Does he always bark?" Ms. Stuart asked.

"It's a speech impediment," Andy quickly explained.

Ruff! Lance in my body barked again.

"On the other hand," Ms. Stuart said, "a career in custodial work might be just the right thing for him."

"We'll be sure to keep that in mind," Andy said. I felt another lurch as we started to move again.

A little while later the drum lid slid off and I squinted up into the bright daylight. Andy's head appeared over the edge of the drum.

"How are you doing, Jake?" he asked.

Arf! I barked.

"I'm gonna tilt the drum over so you can get out," Andy said.

I felt the drum go over, and trotted out. We were in Andy's backyard. Lance, in my body, was lying in the sun. His eyes were closed. He was sleeping.

"I guess all the excitement must have tired him

out," Josh said as he pulled off the dark green coveralls. "Should we get him out of the custodian's uniform?"

"We can leave him in it," Andy said as he got out of his coveralls. "I'm going to take Lance and go find Mica. You take Jake back to your house and wait for us."

"No way." Josh shook his head. "Last time Lance came to my house he chewed up the leg of my mother's coffee table. I don't care where we go, but we're not going home."

"Well, you can't stay here," Andy said. "You're not allowed in the house if I'm not here."

Both Josh and Andy looked stumped for a moment. Then Josh brightened. "I know! I'll take him back to his house. That way he can chew up his own furniture."

"Good idea," Andy said. Then he turned to me. "Come on, Lance, I mean Jake, it's time to find Mica."

15

Josh headed toward my house with Lance in my body. He got him to walk by holding the collar of the custodian's uniform. Andy and I headed toward The Holey Donut. We were walking down the sidewalk when a police car pulled up on the street beside us and its flashing red lights went on!

Andy and I looked around, but we didn't see any criminals or speeders. In fact, we didn't see anyone at all! We were the only people around.

The policeman rolled down his window. It was Officer Parsons, the officer who almost arrested Andy when Lance was in *his* body.

"Hey, Officer Parsons, what's up?" Andy asked.

"Is that your dog, Andy?" Officer Parsons asked.

"Uh, no, it's Jake, Lance Sherman's dog," Andy said.

Officer Parsons frowned. "Lance Sherman? I've never heard of him."

"Oh, uh, I got mixed up," Andy said. "*This* is Lance. He's Jake Sherman's dog."

"I see," Officer Parsons said. "What are you doing with him?"

"I'm just taking him for a walk," Andy said.

"Jake didn't tell you about the new leash law?" Officer Parsons asked.

Oops! We'd forgotten!

"Oh, uh, yeah, I just forgot. Sorry." Andy searched his pockets and came up with Lance's leash, which he clipped onto my collar.

Officer Parsons nodded. "That's better. You wouldn't want Lance to wind up in the animal shelter, would you?"

"No way, Officer Parsons," Andy said.

"Good," said the police officer. "Have a good day." He rolled up his window and drove away.

Andy and I continued on our walk. The world from a dog's point of view sure was different. Mostly knees, bicycle wheels, and babies in strollers.

But the most amazing thing was the smells. There were millions of them! Bitter smells, sweet smells, sour and rotten smells. The smell of leaves, flowers, grass, car exhaust, rubber tires, metal, and plastic. All sorts of things that I'd never noticed before now had scents.

There were so many, in fact, that it was hard to make sense of all the scents!

We had turned a corner and were walking

along a sidewalk past some houses, when out of the corner of my eye I thought I saw something dart behind a tree. A second later the most irresistible scent reached my nose. It was a nutty, furry scent, like nothing I'd ever smelled before.

Groof! The next thing I knew, I let out a bark and raced toward the tree. I must have caught Andy by surprise because I yanked the leash right out of his hand.

"Hey! Come back here!" Andy shouted behind me. But I couldn't help myself. I just *had* to see where that smell was coming from.

I got to the tree and stood against it with my front paws on the trunk. That irresistible, nutty, furry smell was coming from above, but I couldn't see where.

"Geez, I can't believe you," Andy grumbled as he came up behind me. "What are you chasing squirrels for? Don't you know you're not a dog?"

I knew he was right, but I couldn't help myself. The scent was simply *irresistible*!

"Well, forget it," Andy said, picking up the leash. "That squirrel's gone. Let's go."

Andy gave the leash a tug and I followed him back to the sidewalk. We'd just started walking again when suddenly Andy froze.

"Oh, my gosh!" he gasped. "There she is!"

Across the street on the next block, Mica was walking toward us with her dog.

"Maybe we ought to go *this* way." Andy turned

and started walking me in the opposite direction!

That made no sense. I dug my feet, I mean, paws, into the sidewalk and pulled back. Why would Andy go in the opposite direction? He wasn't supposed to go *away* from Mica, he was supposed to go *toward* her.

"Hey, come on." Andy yanked on the leash, but I didn't budge. Andy tugged again. When I still wouldn't move, he kneeled in front of me.

"Don't do this to me, Lance, I mean Jake," he begged desperately. "I know I'm supposed to meet her, but I didn't expect to see her this soon. I'm not ready." He stood up and tugged on the leash. "Come on, please?"

Groof! I barked and shook my, I mean, Lance's head. I didn't change bodies with my dog just so Andy could chicken out.

"Okay, have it your way," Andy said. He dropped the leash, ran around the corner, and disappeared.

16

I found Andy sitting on the curb about a block away. I sat down beside him and gave him a puzzled look.

"I know what you're thinking," he said. "You're wondering why I ran away. Well, you know all those times I said I took Lance for a walk but he ran away before I could meet Mica?"

Arf! I barked yes.

"That's not what really happened," Andy said with a sigh. "The truth is, I'm the one who always runs away. I really want to meet her, but every time I see her I get so nervous I just can't do it."

I stared at him in disbelief.

Andy nodded sadly. "Yeah, I know what you're thinking," he said. "If Lance wasn't the problem, then why did you have to switch bodies with him?"

Groof! I barked. Exactly.

"I guess I was hoping that if you switched bodies with Lance, maybe somehow you'd *make* me meet Mica," Andy said.

I *couldn't* believe it! I'd gone through all that trouble to become Lance and it wasn't even going to help!

Grrrrr! I was so mad I actually growled at him.

"Hey! Don't growl at me!" Andy's forehead bunched up. "What do you care whether I meet Mica or not? The only thing you care about is getting the nose piece for The Holey Donut Face Puzzle Contest."

Well, that was sort of true. But I was still annoyed. There were probably a lot of other deals I could have made with him to get the nose piece. And those deals wouldn't have meant me switching bodies with my dog.

Meanwhile, Andy sat on the curb, slumped over with his chin in his hands, staring forlornly at the street. "It's hopeless, Jake. I'm *never* going to meet Mica. I'm just too chicken."

Down at the other end of the block I saw Mica stop at the corner with her dog. Suddenly I knew what I had to do: I started to run toward them.

"Hey!" Andy called behind me. "What are you doing?"

17

I was going to see Mica. And if necessary, I was prepared to drag her all the way back to Andy. I was a dog with a mission.

Mica's dog noticed me first. She was one of those little brown yappy things with a pink bow on her head to keep the hair out of her eyes. She looked like your basic dust mop with a nose.

Yap! Yap! Yap! She started to bark as I neared her and Mica. I wasn't worried about her. She was so small she could have run through my, I mean, Lance's legs.

"What is it, Foo-Foo?" Mica asked.

Foo-Foo!? What kind of name was that?

Yap! Yap! Yap! Foo-Foo kept yapping at me. One snarl from me probably would have sent her shrieking for home, but I had other things on my mind.

"Another dog!" Mica smiled when she saw me. "Look, Foo-Foo, his tail is wagging. He's come to play with you!"

Yap! Yap! Yap! Foo-Foo stood up on her hind legs.

Show-off, I thought. Forget it, Foo-Foo, I'm not impressed. Go find another dust mop.

"So who do you belong to?" Mica asked me, looking around for my owner.

Groof! Groof! I turned and pointed at Andy. He had gotten to his feet and was standing down the street, watching us.

"Oh, him." Mica smiled and waved at Andy. "Hi!"

"Uh, hi." From down the street, Andy waved back and started to walk slowly toward us.

All right! I thought. Now we were making a little progress.

Yap! Yap! Yap! Foo-Foo kept yapping at me nonstop. I wished she'd shut up already.

"Oh, stop it, Foo-Foo, you're being a pain." Mica bent down and held out her arms. Foo-Foo jumped into them. Mica stood up, holding her dog in her arms like a doll. Meanwhile, Andy ambled toward us with a goofy look on his face.

"Hi," Mica said. "I'm Mica Channing."

"Uh . . . " Andy opened his mouth but no words came out. He looked like he was in a daze.

"What's your name?" Mica asked.

"Uh . . . I'm Andy Kent," Andy replied. "Sorry about the dog."

"Oh, no, I think it's sweet that he came over to meet Foo-Foo," Mica said. "I just wish Foo-Foo would be nicer."

Andy's head bobbed up and down. It seemed like he didn't know what to say.

"What's his name?" Mica asked.

"Lance," Andy said.

"What kind is he?" Mica asked.

"A dog," Andy replied.

Mica gave him a funny look. "I *know* he's a dog. I meant, what *kind* of dog?"

Andy still had that goofy grin on his face. I had a feeling he was super nervous. "Um, uh, I forget."

Mica frowned. "You don't know what kind of dog you have?"

"Well, er, actually, he's my friend's dog," Andy explained. "I'm just using him."

"*Using* him?" The lines in Mica's forehead deepened. "For what?"

"Oh, uh, umm . . . using him to get some exercise," Andy said. "You see, we run together."

"Oh, that's really nice," Mica said. "These dogs need a lot of exercise. Is he friendly?"

"Who?" Andy asked.

"Lance," Mica said.

"Oh, uh, yeah, he's really friendly," Andy said. "In fact, he's one of my best friends."

Mica gave Andy a strange look, but must've decided not to ask what he meant. "Foo-Foo's not very friendly," she said. "I always wish I could get her to play with other dogs, but she never wants to."

"Why don't you give it a try right now?" Andy asked.

Mica thought about it. "Okay, why not?" She looked down at Foo-Foo in her arms. "If I put you down, will you be friendly to Lance?"

Yap! Yap! Foo-Foo yapped and panted with her mouth open. Her little legs bicycled in the air as if she couldn't wait to get down.

I stopped wagging my, I mean, Lance's tail. Frankly, the *last* thing in the world I wanted to do was play with little Miss Dust Mop. But if it would help Andy get to know Mica, I figured it was probably worth it.

Mica put Foo-Foo down.

Yap! Yap! Yap! She instantly started yapping at me again.

What a pain! I was half-tempted to kick her into the nearest sewer drain.

Mica shook her head wistfully. "This is the problem. Foo-Foo doesn't know how to be friendly."

She bent down and held out her arms. But instead of jumping into them, Foo-Foo started to race in a circle around me. *Yap! Yap! Yap!* She was still yapping like crazy. Not only was I starting to get a headache from all the noise, but I was dizzy from moving my head around in circles.

Mica frowned. "That's strange. Usually she jumps right into my arms because she thinks I'm going to protect her."

Foo-Foo stopped running around and faced me. *Yap! Yap! Yap!* At one end, her mouth was yapping nonstop. At the other end, her bushy little tail whipped back and forth like a windshield wiper on overdrive.

Mica looked startled. "I don't believe it! Foo-Foo's wagging her tail! Do you know what that means?"

"She's a dog?" Andy guessed.

"No, silly," Mica said. "It means she *likes* Lance!"

18

Huh? I bent my, I mean, Lance's head and took a closer look at Foo-Foo. She stopped barking and looked up at me with her mouth open and her tongue hanging out.

She was smiling!

Her eyes were sparkling.

Yap! Yap! Yap! she barked.

But it wasn't an angry bark . . . it was an *affectionate* bark!

"I've never seen her like this," Mica picked up Foo-Foo and held her close to my, I mean, Lance's face.

Then Foo-Foo licked my nose!

Gross!

"She kissed him!" Mica cried. "I don't believe it! Foo-Foo's in love!"

Wait a minute!

Foo-Foo wasn't supposed to fall in love with *me*!

Mica was supposed to fall in love with Andy!

Everything was backward!

Mica put Foo-Foo down. The little dust mop stared up at me with love in her eyes. Instead of yapping, she made this cooing sort of sound. Then she stood up on her hind legs and stuck out her tongue!

She wanted to kiss again!

I started to back away. Nope! No way! This wasn't part of the deal. I looked up at Andy, hoping he'd understand my problem and leave.

But Andy was talking to Mica. They chuckled over something. Andy was acting like he didn't even know I was there! He'd completely forgotten about me!

Groof! I barked to get his attention.

Andy didn't blink.

Groof! Groof! I barked louder.

Andy looked down at me. "Not now, Jake."

"Jake?" Mica frowned. "I thought you said his name was Lance."

"Oh, uh, it is Lance," Andy said. "Jake is just his nickname."

"Isn't that an odd nickname for a dog named Lance," Mica asked.

"Yeah, well, Lance is an odd dog," Andy replied.

I felt something brush against my back leg. I looked down. It was Foo-Foo! Purring like a kitten and rubbing against my leg!

Geez, what was wrong with that dog?

Grr. . . . I snarled at her.

Foo-Foo backed away and whined unhappily.

"Uh-oh," Mica said. "I think we have a problem."

"What?" Andy appeared to be caught by surprise.

"Foo-Foo and Lance aren't getting along," Mica said. "Foo-Foo likes Lance, but I'm not sure Lance likes Foo-Foo."

"Let me talk to Lance for a second." Andy slid his hand under my, I mean, Lance's collar, and led me down the sidewalk. Then he squatted down until he was eye-to-eye with me.

"What's this about you not getting along with Foo-Foo?" he whispered.

Groof! I barked.

"I don't care whether you like her or not," Andy hissed. "The only way you're going to get my Holey Donut nose piece and have a chance to win the home entertainment center is if you play along. Get it?"

I looked over Andy's shoulder at Foo-Foo. She gazed back at me with loving eyes. I felt ill inside.

"Now, go on," Andy whispered. "Go show little miss Foo-Foo what a gentleman you can be."

Andy started to lead me back to Mica and Foo-Foo. I couldn't believe it! How had I gotten myself into this mess? This wasn't supposed to be a double date!

"Oh, there you are, Andy!" a voice suddenly said. "I'm so glad I found you!"

19

We turned around. My sister, Jessica, was coming up the sidewalk toward us. She had so much black makeup around her eyes she looked like a raccoon.

"Oh, uh, hi, Jessica," Andy said. He introduced her to Mica. Jessica told Mica it was nice to meet her and what a cute little dog Foo-Foo was. Then she turned back to Andy.

"I have to take Lance," she said.

"Where?" Andy asked.

"To obedience school," Jessica said. "I managed to get him into a class that starts in about twenty minutes. This is my last chance to teach him to stay out of the garbage."

"Which obedience school are you going to?" Mica asked.

"The one Mrs. Pudlhafer runs in the church basement," Jessica said.

"Oh, wow," said Mica. "What a coincidence! That's where we're going, too."

"Why are you taking Foo-Foo to obedience school?" Andy asked.

"She wakes me up every morning at five o'clock," Mica explained. "I'm trying to teach her to stop."

"Then we can go together," Jessica said.

Yap! Yap! Yap! Foo-Foo barked happily and gave me that gooey-eyed, love-puppy look.

Now I had to go to obedience school with her?

If Jessica was going to take Lance, I mean, me to obedience school, that didn't leave anything for Andy to do.

"Well, uh, it was really nice to meet you," he said to Mica.

"It was nice meeting you, too," Mica replied.

Andy looked down and scuffed his shoe against the sidewalk. It was pretty obvious that he didn't want to leave. "So, uh, maybe I'll see you around sometime."

"Sure," said Mica. "I'd love to get Foo-Foo together with Lance again. I'm so glad Foo-Foo has finally found a friend."

"Oh, yeah, definitely." Andy smiled. I could see he was looking forward to walking Lance again. That was okay with me, as long as Lance was back in Lance's body and I was back in mine.

"So, uh, I guess this is good-bye for now," Andy said and started to walk away. I trotted alongside him.

"Lance!" Jessica called out. "Where do you think you're going?"

I was going with Andy. I was going to get back into my old body. *That's* where I was going.

Andy stopped and looked down at me. "You can't come with me. You have to go to obedience school."

Groof! I barked back. He couldn't be serious. I didn't need obedience school, Lance did.

Andy kneeled down until we were face-to-face. "Don't you get it, Jake?" he whispered. "You *have* to go to obedience school. If you don't, your father is going to get rid of Lance."

Groof! I shook Lance's head. That wasn't *my* problem.

"You still don't get it, do you?" Andy said. "If your father gets rid of Lance, then I can't walk him anymore. And if I can't walk him anymore, then I won't have an excuse to meet Mica again. And if I can't meet Mica again, you don't get the nose for The Holey Donut Face Puzzle Contest."

Groof! Groof! I barked angrily. That wasn't fair. I'd lived up to my half of the deal! I'd helped Andy meet Mica. That was all I was supposed to do!

But Andy just shook his head slowly back and forth and whispered, "Tough noogies, Jake."

20

A few moments later, I was walking with Jessica, Mica, and Foo-Foo toward the church. Foo-Foo trotted along beside me. She had to take about six steps for each one I took, and she never took those gooey, love-puppy eyes off me.

Mica and Jessica giggled all the way to the church.

"I can't get over Foo-Foo," Mica said. "I've *never* seen her act this way. She usually *hates* other dogs."

"It's so adorable seeing them together," Jessica agreed.

Adorable? I wanted to barf!

"Has Lance ever been to obedience school before?" Mica asked.

"Once," Jessica replied. "In fact, it was to Mrs. Pudlhafer's class. It was really strange because as soon as he got into class, Lance did *exactly* what he was supposed to do. In fact, he did things I didn't even know he *could* do!"

"So what happened?" Mica asked.

"Mrs. Pudlhafer thought I brought a trained dog to class just to make fun of the other dogs," Jessica said. "She threw us out."

What Jessica didn't know was that she hadn't brought Lance to obedience school. She'd brought Andy in Lance's body. All my sister knew was that for a brief time Lance behaved more like a human than a dog. Then, after Andy and Lance switched back to their own bodies, Lance started being a dog again and did dumb dog stuff like get into the garbage.

"Aren't you worried that Mrs. Pudlhafer will remember you?" Mica asked.

"I'm hoping she won't," Jessica said. "She must see so many dogs. I'm praying she'll think Lance is just another yellow Lab."

"You're probably right," Mica agreed. "She must see hundreds of dogs."

We got to the church and went down the back stairs to the basement. The room had been cleared of tables and chairs. Small orange plastic cones marked off a large square on the floor.

Spread around the room were about a dozen people, each with a dog. The dogs came in every possible size and shape, and they were all barking and howling and tugging at their leashes as they tried to get to the other dogs.

The last time we'd been here, Andy in Lance's body had been the exception. While all the other

60

dogs barked and pulled at their leashes, he'd sat perfectly still.

This time I barked and tugged at my leash, trying to act like any other dog. Meanwhile, Foo-Foo, Miss Little Chicken Dog, hid behind me and whimpered.

"Isn't that sweet?" Mica gushed. "Lance thinks he's protecting his girlfriend."

My *girlfriend*? Hey, wait a minute! That's not what I was doing! I was just trying to act like any other dumb dog.

Mrs. Pudlhafer came into the basement. She was a thin lady who wore jeans and a pink T-shirt with a silhouette of a poodle on it. Her curly white hair even looked like poodle hair. I remembered that the last time we were there I'd nicknamed her Ms. Poodlehair.

Ms. Poodlehair went around the room giving out shiny chain choke collars to the dog owners. "Welcome to canine obedience school," she said. "It's always so nice to see all these new faces."

But when she got to Jessica and me, Ms. Poodlehair stopped and frowned.

I held my breath.

Gulp! Jessica swallowed nervously.

"Don't I know you?" Ms. Poodlehair asked.

21

My sister fidgeted with her earrings. "I don't think so."

"That's funny," Ms. Poodlehair said. "You look very familiar. And so does your dog. I never forget a name. What's his name?"

"Uh . . . " Jessica hesitated. She must've been afraid that if she said "Lance" Ms. Poodlehair would remember. Just then a small woman with a large brown and white Great Dane came into the church basement. All the other dogs started to bark.

Ms. Poodlehair turned away. "Bring your dog over here and I'll help you get him settled down."

Meanwhile, Jessica glanced nervously at Mica.

"Call him by his nickname," Mica whispered.

"Lance doesn't have a nickname," Jessica whispered back.

"Andy said his nickname was Jake," Mica whispered.

"No, that's my brother's name," said Jessica.

"Well, Andy called him Jake and Lance seemed to know what he meant," Mica said.

By now Ms. Poodlehair had gotten the lady with the Great Dane settled. She came back toward Jessica and me.

"Now where were we?" she said, putting her hands on her hips and staring down at me. "Your dog's name is . . . ?"

"Jake," Jessica replied.

"Jake." Ms. Poodlehair rubbed her chin. "No, I don't recall a Lab with that name. Sorry, I guess I was mistaken."

Phew! Jessica and I both breathed a sigh of relief.

But the relief didn't last for long. Not only was I trapped in Lance's body, I was trapped in obedience school as well! When Jessica told Ms. Poodlehair that my problem was getting into the garbage, she said she had a lot of experience with that problem. She took Jessica and me over to a garbage can like the one we had in our kitchen.

"As you can see, this garbage can has dog biscuits in it," Ms. Poodlehair said. "Jake is going to be very interested in it. But every time he goes near it, you give him a good smack on the nose with this."

Ms. Poodlehair handed Jessica a rolled-up newspaper.

My sister looked shocked. "But won't that *hurt?*"

63

"Of course it'll hurt," Ms. Poodlehair replied. "How else are you going to teach that dumb mutt to stay out of the garbage?"

"But what about his *feelings*?" Jessica asked.

"Feelings?" Ms. Poodlehair laughed. "He's a dog for Pete's sake. What are you worried about his feelings for?"

Jessica dropped the rolled-up newspaper and backed away, shaking her head. "I'm sorry, but I think coming here was a mistake. I think I better go."

"And I'm going, too," said Mica. She grabbed Foo-Foo's leash and followed Jessica and me out of the church basement.

"Sure, go ahead!" Ms. Poodlehair yelled after us. "Go read those silly books on dog psychology. Then sit down with your dogs and have a talk! I bet they'll have plenty to say!"

22

Jessica, Mica, Foo-Foo, and I climbed out of the church basement.

"Could you believe her?" Mica asked. "I bet if I told her about my problem, she would have told me to gag Foo-Foo and lock her in the closet at night."

Jessica nodded. "She's totally out of touch with what it's like to be a dog."

Maybe Ms. Poodlehair was out of touch, but I sure wasn't. I knew exactly how it felt to be a dog. And I didn't particularly like it. Outside the church, Foo-Foo was still following me around with that dumb, love-puppy look on her face. Gee, didn't she have *any* self-respect?

"I guess I better take Lance home," Jessica said to Mica. "It was nice meeting you."

"Nice meeting you, too," Mica said. "And I'm really glad Foo-Foo got to meet Lance. Let's get them together again soon."

Over Lance's dead body! I thought.

"Definitely," Jessica said. "We're always around. We're bound to run into each other." She waved good-bye and we started down the sidewalk.

We hadn't gone very far when I heard rapid footsteps behind us. I turned and saw Andy jogging to catch up to us.

Jessica turned. "Oh, hi, Andy."

"Hi, Jessica," Andy said. "How was obedience school?"

"Horrible," my sister said. "The lady who runs it is completely out of touch with the canine sensibility. But you know what was weird? Mica said you told her Lance's nickname was Jake. What was that all about?"

"Uh, gee, I don't know." Andy played dumb. "I might have said your brother's name is Jake. Maybe she got it mixed up."

"Maybe," Jessica said. "Anyway, where are you going?"

"I thought I'd go to your house," Andy said. "I want to see what Jake's up to."

Neither Andy nor Jessica said much for the rest of the walk home. I was glad to get away from Foo-Foo, and I was really looking forward to getting back into my own body. I'd definitely completed my part of the deal. Now it was time to switch bodies with Lance, get the nose piece for The Holey Donut Face Puzzle Contest, and see if

I could win that home entertainment center.

It wasn't long before we got to my house and went up the front walk. Jessica stopped at the front door and unlocked it. She was just pushing the door open when Josh's voice rang out from the kitchen: "Oh, no! Jake, look what you've done!"

23

Jessica hurried into the kitchen. Andy and I followed. Josh was standing in the middle of the kitchen with his back toward us. He didn't know we were there.

The kitchen floor was a *mess*! It was covered with garbage.

Lance, in my body, was on his hands and knees crawling around in it!

"What is going on?" Jessica gasped.

Josh spun around and looked surprised. "Jessica! Andy! What are you doing here?"

"We just came back from obedience school," Jessica said. "Why is the kitchen floor covered with garbage? Why is my brother crawling around in it? What's that outfit he's wearing?"

As soon as Lance, in my body, heard my sister's voice, he crawled into a corner and cowered with a really guilty look on his face.

"Uh, well, that's a good question, Jessica," Josh said, biting his lip nervously. "In fact, it's a *really* good question. Don't you think so, Andy?"

"Oh, yeah," Andy agreed. "It's an excellent question. In fact, it's one of the best questions I've ever heard. I mean, it's even *better* than excellent."

"It's so good it probably qualifies for the Question Hall of Fame," said Josh.

"You're right, Josh," Andy said. "It *definitely* qualifies for the Question Hall of Fame. It's right up there with 'Why is the sky blue?' and 'How does a Thermos know to keep iced tea cold and hot tea hot?'"

Jessica smirked. "I have news for you, guys. I'm not amused. Now somebody better tell me why the floor is covered with garbage and why my brother was crawling around in it. In fact, why doesn't Jake tell us himself?"

Andy and Josh stared at each other in horror. How long would it take before Jessica figured out why I, I mean, Lance in my body, was unable to answer?

24

"You don't have to ask him," Josh gasped. "I can tell you."

"Okay." Jessica put her hands on her hips and waited.

"Well, you see," Josh began, "the garbage is on the floor because . . . er . . . uh . . ."

"You put it there on purpose," Andy said.

"That's right!" Josh said.

"Why?" asked Jessica.

"Why . . . what?" Josh asked back.

"Why would you scatter the garbage all over the floor?"

"Uh . . . because . . . uh . . . er . . ." Josh gave Andy a pleading look.

"You were looking for something," Andy said.

"That's it!" Josh said. "We were looking for something."

"But why were you looking for it in the garbage?" Jessica asked.

"Uh . . . er . . ." Josh stammered.

"Because they accidentally threw it out," Andy said.

"Threw what out?" asked Jessica.

"Yeah, Andy," said Josh. "Just what did we throw out?"

"Uh . . . er . . ." Now it was Andy's turn to hem and haw.

"Wait a minute," Jessica said. "Why are you asking Andy? He wasn't even here."

"Yeah, Josh," Andy gloated. "Try coming up with some answers yourself."

"Why should I?" Josh snapped back. "You're doing such a good job of it."

"It's not that hard," Andy shot back. "Anyone with a brain bigger than a peanut should be able to think of an answer."

"Oh, yeah?" huffed Josh. "If I have a peanut brain, you've got no brain at all!"

"Look who's talking!" Andy cried. "You're so dumb the mind reader gave you a fifty percent discount!"

"Oh, yeah?" Josh said. "Well, you're so dumb you put your watch in the bank to save time."

"Oh, really?" Andy scoffed. "Well, you're so stupid you had to stick your head in a microwave to get a hot idea."

"That's nothing," cried Josh. "You're so thick you left your brain to science but they wouldn't take it."

"Oh, yeah!" shouted Andy. "Well — "

"SHUT UP!" Jessica screamed. Her face was red. "As far as I'm concerned, you're both idiots! All I want to know is why there's garbage all over the kitchen floor! And the person who really should be telling me is my jerk-brain brother."

We all looked around for Lance in my body, but he was no longer in the corner. Now he was lying under the kitchen table, asleep.

"Jake?" Jessica said.

Lance in my body didn't budge.

"Oh, my gosh!" Jessica suddenly gasped. "I know what he's doing! He's being weird!" She bent down. "Okay, Jake, congratulations. You've finally done it. You've proved that you can be weird, too. Now do me a favor and clean up the kitchen, okay?"

Lance in my body still didn't move. Jessica kneeled closer. It looked like she was going to grab his shoulder and shake him.

"I wouldn't do that," Josh warned her.

Jessica looked back at him. "Why not?"

"It's best to let sleeping dogs lie," Andy said.

Jessica scowled. "What are you talking about, Andy? That's not a sleeping dog, that's — "

Suddenly my sister's eyes widened and her jaw dropped. She knew about Mr. Dirksen's machine. In fact, it wasn't so long ago that she and I used it to switch bodies.

"Wait a minute!" she cried. "You didn't switch

them, did you? Not Lance and Jake! Tell me you didn't!"

"Of course, we didn't," Josh said, then glowered at Andy for opening his big mouth.

"Yeah, that's not what I meant when I said to let sleeping dogs lie," Andy said. "It was just a joke."

But it was obvious Jessica didn't believe him. She came over to me in Lance's body and kneeled down. Then she stared right into my, I mean, Lance's eyes. "Lance? Jake? Who's in there?"

I knew I had to act like Lance. *Groof!* I barked and panted with my tongue hanging out.

But my sister didn't look convinced. "Sorry, that's too easy. Either of you could have done that." She ran her hand over her super-short hair and thought for a moment. "Let's see," she said to herself. "There has to be a way to figure out whether my brother is just *acting* weird or has switched bodies with my dog. What's something that Lance would do that Jake would *never* do?"

"Take a bath?" Andy suggested.

"That sounds more like something *you'd* never do," Jessica replied.

"Two points!" Josh licked his fingers and scored an imaginary two in the air.

"I don't know what you think is so funny, Josh," Jessica warned him. "If I find out you switched Jake with Lance, you're *all* dead, understand?"

Josh swallowed nervously and nodded. Meanwhile, Lance in my body continued to sleep under the kitchen table. Jessica looked around the kitchen. Suddenly a big smile appeared on her face. "I know just the thing!"

25

"Dog food?" Josh made a face.

"The best dog food made," Jessica said with a smile. *"Canine Connoisseur.* Lance loves it."

I watched dismally as my sister filled Lance's bowl with those disgusting, smelly brown pellets made from beef, chicken, and fish by-products.

Chicken brains . . .

Cow eyeballs . . .

Fish noses . . .

"If you're really Lance," Jessica said to me, "you're going to love this."

I went over and stared down at the pellets in the bowl. The smell made me want to barf. What if one of those pellets had a chicken eyeball in it? Or a fish brain!

Gross!

"Well?" Jessica crossed her arms and tapped her foot. "I'm waiting."

I knew I had no choice. This was going to be the worst, most disgusting thing I'd ever done! If

I didn't win that complete home entertainment center after this I'd —

"*Owwwwwwwwoooooooooooo!*" Suddenly the most aching, lovesick dog howl I'd ever heard floated in through the open kitchen window.

Jessica spun around. "What in the world was that?"

26

Jessica headed toward the front door, but Josh, Andy, and I stayed behind in the kitchen.

"We almost got caught," Andy said.

"What do you mean, almost?" said Josh. "As soon as she comes back, Lance is either gonna eat that dog food or we're dead."

As Josh said that, he and Andy stared down at me in Lance's body.

Gruff! I shook Lance's head. Forget it. There was no way I was going to eat that stuff.

"Guess again, Jake," Josh said. "What do you think your sister's going to do to us if she finds out we switched you with her big, furry love puppy?"

"Talk about a fate totally worse than death," Andy said.

I stared down at the bowl of *Canine Connoisseur* pellets again.

Fish eyes . . .

Chicken noses . . .

Wait a minute! Did chickens even *have* noses?

"Oh, Lance!" Jessica called from the front door. "Lancy pooh, there's someone here to see you!"

I looked up. Josh and Andy traded a puzzled glance.

"Now what?" Andy asked.

"Let's go see," Josh said. "At least we'll get out of the kitchen."

I followed Josh and Andy to the front door. Jessica was kneeling in the doorway. It looked like she was talking to someone or something, but I couldn't see who.

"Oh, Lancy pooh." Jessica turned and gave me a big smile. "Look who came to see you."

She stood up and moved out of the way.

Standing outside the front door was Foo-Foo!

27

The little dust mop looked up at me with those gooey, love-puppy eyes.

"And look!" Jessica pointed down at the front walk. "She brought you a present!"

Lying on the walk was a soggy-looking dog biscuit covered with dog slobber.

"Isn't that sweet?" Jessica gushed.

Sweet? It was the grossest, most repulsive thing I'd ever seen. It even made those *Canine Connoisseur* pellets look good!

"Why don't I take you both out to the backyard and let you get to know each other in private?" Jessica said. It seemed that for the moment she'd forgotten who might be in her love puppy's body.

"Uh, I hate to say this," Andy interrupted. "I think it's really nice that Foo-Foo came over to see Lance, but I wonder if Mica knows. I mean, Foo-Foo never goes anywhere without Mica. She might discover that Foo-Foo's missing and totally freak out."

"You're right," Jessica said. "We better take Foo-Foo back to her house."

"I'll do it," Andy volunteered.

"Lance and I'll go, too," Josh said.

Jessica blinked. Her smile disappeared and she pressed her lips into a hard, flat line. "Not so fast. First we're going to see if Lance ate his dog food. Andy, you can take Foo-Foo home. But Lance and Josh are coming with me back to the kitchen."

Josh and I had no choice but to follow Jessica. This time I knew I was a dead dog.

28

We all went into the kitchen.

"I don't believe it!" Jessica gasped.

Josh and I looked in the bowl. Those disgusting *Canine Connoisseur* pellets were gone!

We looked around. Lance in my body was still asleep under the kitchen table!

"Well, I guess I owe you an apology, Josh," Jessica said. "I was totally certain that you'd switched Jake with Lance. Why didn't you tell me Lance ate his dog food?"

"Uh . . ." Josh didn't know what to say.

"He must have eaten it when I went to the door to see who was howling," Jessica said.

Josh nodded dumbly and looked under the kitchen table again. Lance in my body was lying on the floor with his eyes closed and a big smile on his face.

"I guess that's just Jake being extra weird," Jessica said with a sigh.

Brinnnggg! From upstairs came the sound of a phone ringing. "That's mine," Jessica said and hurried out of the kitchen.

As soon as she left, Josh went over to Lance's bowl. He picked it up to see if the food was hidden under it.

But the *Canine Connoisseur* pellets were gone.

"I don't get it," Josh said, scratching his head. "Where'd the dog food go?"

Just then Lance in my body rolled over under the kitchen table. *Urrrp!* In his sleep he burped and licked his lips, then smiled again.

Josh blinked. Then his eyes went wide. "Oh, no!" He turned to me. "*You* ate it, Jake! I mean, Lance in your body ate it! He must've woken up, eaten the dog food, then gone back to sleep!"

I looked at the empty bowl, then at Lance in my body under the table. *Gross!* I felt totally sick! I wanted to barf. Lance in my body had eaten that whole bowl of dog food. Those disgusting brown pellets were now in my body's stomach!

Triple-Mega-Gross!

"I know it's totally disgusting," Josh said. "But we're also really lucky. If Jake, I mean, Lance hadn't eaten that stuff, we would have been busted."

I can't say that made me feel any better. In a few hours I was supposed to get back into my body again. And when I did, I'd have a stomach full of half-digested dog food!

"All we have to do is wait for Andy to get back from Mica's house," Josh said.

"Then we'll go over to school and switch you and Lance back. Andy'll give you the nose piece, and he'll give me the fifth issue of Mole Man. We'll all have what we wanted."

And I'd have something I didn't want — a stomach full of dog food.

We heard footsteps racing down the stairs. Jessica dashed into the kitchen breathlessly. "That was Kirk Stone! He wanted to know if I felt like going to the mall! He's going to be here in five minutes! I have to go fix my makeup! Will you watch Lance for me until I get back?"

Josh nodded.

"Great! Thanks a bunch! Bye!" She spun around and ran upstairs to get ready.

"I can't believe there's a guy who actually likes her," Josh said in amazement.

Arf! I barked and nodded in agreement.

Josh shook his head. "I bet he's a real dog, too."

Rrrrr. . . . Behind us Lance in my body stretched and got up on his hands and knees. He yawned, then crawled over to the kitchen door. He scratched at it with his hand. Then he turned and looked at Josh over his shoulder. Then he scratched at the door again.

Josh gave me a weary look. "Does that mean what I *think* it means?"

Arf! I nodded Lance's head.

"Why me?" Josh groaned.

29

"Ready?" Josh asked. We were standing by the kitchen door. Josh was holding the collar of the green coveralls so that Lance in my body would walk and not crawl.

Josh opened the kitchen door.

Lance in my body immediately got down on his hands and knees.

"No, you can't do that," Josh said and tried to pull Lance in my body to his feet.

But Lance in my body refused to stand. Every time Josh pulled him up, he'd get back down on his hands and knees.

"I don't get it," Josh said. "When Lance was in Andy's body, he stood up. He stood up this morning when we left school. Why won't he stand up now?"

I didn't know the answer. And even if I did, I wouldn't have been able to explain it. For whatever reason, Lance didn't want to stand.

"This isn't going to work," Josh said. "Lance

has to go out. But he's in your body, Jake. I can't take him out on his hands and knees. It'll look ridiculous."

I didn't care how ridiculous it might look, but I was worried that it would *hurt!* My knees and hands weren't padded like a dog's paws. They weren't made to go crawling along sidewalks and across streets.

Groof! Suddenly I had an idea and trotted down the front hall to the closet where we kept our Rollerblading stuff.

"Now where are *you* going?" Josh called after me.

I stuck my, I mean, Lance's head in the closet. *Darn it!* It was dark and filled with junk. And in Lance's body, there was no way I could reach the light switch. How was I going to find what I was looking for?

Sniff!

Wait a minute. Maybe I couldn't *see* anything, but I could sure *smell* it! I squeezed further into the dark closet and sniffed around. It was amazing! I could smell everything! Baseball gloves, soccer cleats, softballs, footballs.

It wasn't long before I found what I was looking for. I picked it up in Lance's mouth and trotted back into the kitchen where I dropped it at Josh's feet.

Josh frowned. "A plastic knee guard? What am I supposed to do with this? Go Rollerblading?"

Groff! I barked and hurried back to the front closet. In short order I returned with another plastic knee guard and two metal hand protectors.

Josh shook his head wearily. "You expect me to put this stuff on Lance, I mean, on you?"

Arf! I barked yes. Then I thought of something else and left.

When I returned, Josh had already gotten the knee and hand protectors on Lance in my body. Now I dropped Lance's leash at his feet.

"For Lance?" Josh asked.

Groof! I shook Lance's head.

"For you!" Josh guessed. "Because of the leash law."

Arf! I barked yes.

Josh clipped the leash to my collar. "Happy now?"

Arf! I barked.

Ruff! Ruff! Meanwhile, Lance in my body was on his hands and knees, wearing the knee and hand protectors and pawing at the kitchen door to get out.

"Okay, okay, chill out," Josh said, pulling open the door. Lance in my body bounded out on his hands and knees.

Josh picked up the leash and we followed.

"Here goes nothing," Josh moaned.

30

Lance had his favorite places. And Lance in my body was no different. Soon we were following him down the sidewalk. It should have been a typical scene of two boys walking a dog. But in this case, one of the boys led the way on his hands and knees.

Drivers in cars and kids on bikes slowed down to stare at us. The people we passed on the sidewalk stopped and scowled.

"I can't believe I'm doing this!" Josh grumbled under his breath.

Just then that irresistible, nutty, furry scent wafted toward us. Across the street, a squirrel darted into a small park. The next thing I knew, Lance, in my body, stopped and became alert!

"No! Jake, I mean, Lance!" Josh shouted.

But Lance in my body shot across the street after the squirrel.

And right into the path of a car!

31

Screeech! The driver slammed on his brakes and just barely missed hitting me, I mean, Lance in my body! Meanwhile, Lance in my body scampered across the sidewalk on his hands and knees and into a park.

"Stop!" Josh yelled.

Groof! I barked.

We both ran into the street to follow him. By now the driver of the car opened the door and got out. He was a tall, bald man.

"What in the world is going on?" he asked.

"It's really hard to explain," Josh yelled as we followed Lance in my body into the park.

"I'll bet!" the driver yelled back.

The park had a sandbox, some swings, and a slide. A bunch of little kids were playing in the sandbox while their mothers sat on a bench and talked.

But no one was talking. They were all staring at Lance in my body, who was pressed against a tree, scratching at the trunk and barking. *Ruff! Ruff!* To anyone who didn't know what was going on, it looked like a boy in dark green coveralls was scratching at the tree trunk and barking.

The mothers got off the bench and started gathering their children around them.

"What's that boy doing, Mommy?" one of the little kids asked.

"It's okay, everyone!" Josh called as he jogged toward Lance in my body. "Really, nothing to worry about. Everything's fine."

Ruff! Ruff! Lance in my body barked up the tree again.

"What *is* he doing?" one of the mothers asked.

"He's, uh, checking the tree," Josh said.

"Checking it for what?" asked the mother.

"Uh, bats."

"*Bats!*" several mothers gasped, alarmed.

"Yeah, if you bark at a tree and there are bats in it, they'll fly away," Josh said. He looked up and pointed. "I don't see any bats so I guess everything's fine."

The mothers looked relieved. Meanwhile, Josh grabbed the collar of the green coveralls and started to lead Lance in my body away from the tree.

"Since you're here, don't you think you should check the other trees for bats?" one of the mothers asked.

"Oh, it's not necessary," Josh said. "We've determined that this area is bat-free."

"Then thank you very much," said another mother.

"No sweat," Josh said.

We headed back toward the sidewalk. "I can't believe what a liar I am," Josh muttered. "I ought to be inducted into the Fat Fib Hall of Fame."

Ruff! Lance in my body barked again as another squirrel darted across our path. He lurched after the squirrel, but this time Josh held him back by the collar of the coveralls.

"This is ridiculous," Josh complained. "I can't hold onto him like this."

He looked around as if trying to figure out what to do. Then his eyes settled on me. "Come here, Lance, I mean, Jake."

I went over. Josh put his hands around my, I mean, Lance's neck and unbuckled the dog collar.

Gruff! I shook my head in protest. What about the leash law?

"Forget it, Jake," Josh grumbled as he clipped the dog collar around Lance's, I mean, my neck. "If he's going to act like a dog, he's going to get treated like one."

We started down the sidewalk again. Only now Lance in my body was on the leash.

Gruff! I barked and shook my, I mean, Lance's head again.

"Just chill, Jake," Josh said. "We're going back to your house. Nothing's going to happen."

"*Ahem!*" Someone cleared his throat loudly.

Josh and I stopped and turned.

Officer Parsons was staring at us from his patrol car. The lights were flashing. He nodded at Lance in my body, on his hands and knees, with a dog collar around his neck.

"Tell me I'm seeing things."

Officer Parsons shook his head slowly.

32

J osh swallowed nervously. "Oh, uh, hi, Officer Parsons."

"Hello, Josh," the cop replied. "Maybe you'd like to tell me what's going on."

"Well, uh, we were just going for a walk," Josh said.

"Do you always go for walks with your friends on their hands and knees and with leashes around their necks?" the police officer asked.

"Well . . ." Josh rubbed his chin and gazed up at the sky as if he had to think about it. "Not always."

"I'm glad to hear it," Officer Parsons said. "So what's the story?"

"The story," Josh repeated, biting his lip. "Hmmm . . . oh yeah, the story is . . . there's this new contest called Dog for a Day. And in order to win you have to act like a dog all day."

Ruff! Lance in my body barked and panted with his tongue hanging out.

"Dog for a Day, huh?" Officer Parsons said. "And who is running this contest?"

"Uh, MTV," Josh said.

"No kidding?" said Officer Parsons. "How do you compete? I mean, how do they know that the contestants are really acting like dogs?"

"Well, uh, there are judges everywhere," Josh said. "Except they're in disguise. I hear they're driving around in unmarked vans. Like, you see that Federal Express van?"

Josh pointed at a white FedEx van with big purple and orange letters.

"Sure looks like a FedEx van to me," said Officer Parsons.

"Well, it *might* be," Josh allowed. "Or it might be an MTV Dog for a Day van in disguise. You just never know."

Officer Parsons nodded. "You're right, Josh, you never know. But want to know what I *do* know?"

"Uh, what?" Josh asked.

"I know that Jake may be *acting* like a dog," the officer said, "but there's a *real* dog right next to you and he's in violation of the town's new leash law."

"But — " Josh began.

"No 'buts,' Josh," Officer Parsons said. "You get a leash on that dog, or he goes to the animal shelter."

"Uh, yes, sir," Josh said. "I will, sir."

"Now!" Officer Parsons said.

Josh kneeled down. He took the dog collar off Jake's neck and put it on mine.

Ruff! Lance, in my body, took off into the woods on his hands and knees.

Officer Parsons, Josh, and I watched him disappear.

"Good luck with the contest, Josh," Officer Parsons said and drove away.

33

By the time we found Lance in my body again, it was getting late.

"We better get back to your house fast," Josh said, keeping a firm grip on the collar of the green coveralls so that Lance in my body couldn't run away again. "It's almost time for school to close and we have to get you and Lance switched back into the right bodies. Andy's probably waiting for us. He probably can't figure out where we are."

We got back to my house. Jessica must have been at the mall with that Kirk guy. But Andy wasn't there either.

"I don't get it," Josh said, standing in the front hall. "He knows we have to get you and Lance switched before the teachers' conference ends. Where is he?"

I thought back to the last time we'd seen Andy. He was taking Foo-Foo back to Mica's house.

Mica's house!

Suddenly I knew where Andy was.

Groof! I barked at Josh.

"What?" Josh asked.

Groof! Groof! I barked again.

"What are you trying to say, Jake?' he asked.

Groof! It was so obvious!

"Hey, listen, I'm not a dog, okay?" Josh sounded annoyed. "I don't know what *groof* means."

How could I explain? Maybe he'd get the idea if I tried to sound like Foo-Foo. *Yarp! Yarp!*

Josh looked at me like I was crazy. "What's wrong with you?"

Yarp! Yarp! I tried again. Believe me, it's not easy to yap when you're in the body of an eighty-pound yellow Lab.

"Yarp? Yarp?" Josh repeated and shook his head as if he had no idea what I was trying to say. But then he stopped shaking his head. His eyes widened. "You're right! That *must* be where he is! And we're running out of time! We better go!"

34

A moment later we were lurching down the sidewalk as fast as we could go. Josh held the collar of the coveralls to keep Lance in my body standing. He'd tied my leash to Lance's right hand so I could help pull.

Grrrrrrr . . . . Lance in my body growled. He clearly didn't like standing or being pulled, but that was too bad. We were running out of time.

After several blocks we turned a corner and went down Mica's street. Ahead, we could see Andy and Mica sitting on the front steps of a house, talking.

"Do you believe it!?" Josh whispered hoarsely. "He's just sitting there talking! Like he totally forgot about us."

We stopped in front of them. We were all breathing hard. Andy looked surprised. He smiled awkwardly. "Oh, uh, hi, guys."

"Have we forgotten something?" Josh asked.

Andy glanced out the corner of his eye at Mica.

"Well, uh, we're in the middle of talking. Maybe you guys could come back a little later."

"I don't think so," Josh said.

Andy glanced at Mica again. "Uh, could you excuse me for a moment?"

"Okay," she said.

Andy got up and came down the steps toward us.

Ruff! Ruff! Lance in my body barked at him.

Mica frowned.

Andy spun around to her. "Oh, don't mind Jake. It's just an allergy. It makes him cough."

"It sounded more like a bark than a cough," Mica said.

"Well, yeah, he's allergic to bark," Andy said. "It makes him bark."

Ruff! Ruff! Lance in my body barked again.

"Get him out of here," Andy hissed at Josh.

"No way," Josh hissed back. "You have to come with us to school and help get Jake back into his own body."

Ruff! Ruff! barked Lance in my body.

"Maybe he needs some water," Mica said. "I'll go get him some."

"Great idea," Andy said.

Mica went into her house. Andy turned back to Josh. "I'm serious. You guys have to go. This is a really crucial time. Mica and I are finally talking."

"If you don't come with us right now," Josh

said, "Jake and Lance aren't going to be able to switch back to their own bodies."

"So? Maybe Jake wouldn't mind being a dog for a few more days," Andy said.

I opened Lance's mouth and closed it around Andy's ankle. The *last* thing I wanted to do was be in Lance's body, and I was determined to let Andy know it.

"Uh, I don't think Jake likes that idea," Josh said.

35

As soon as Lance in my body saw me in *his* body with my mouth around Andy's ankle, he crouched down and closed his mouth around Andy's *other* ankle. Now it looked like a dog had one of Andy's ankles and a *boy* had the other.

"Hey!" Andy protested and tried to pull his feet away, but we just clamped down harder. He wasn't going anywhere.

"What's going on?" It was Mica. She'd just come out of the house with a glass of water.

"Oh, uh, nothing." Andy tried to kick his ankles free again, but neither Lance nor I would let go. We were going to hold Andy hostage until he agreed to help us switch back into our own bodies.

Yap! Yap! Yap! Oh, no! Foo-Foo came out the front door and flopped down the front steps, yapping and panting and all excited.

She must've thought I'd come to see her!

Forget this! I let go of Andy's ankle and backed

away. Foo-Foo gave me that gooey, love-puppy look.

I started to run.

Yap! Yap! Yap! Foo-Foo started to follow me.

"Foo-Foo!" Mica started to run after her little dust mop.

"Mica!" Andy started to run after Mica.

"Andy!" Josh started to run after Andy.

I didn't want to leave Mica's property. With my luck I'd head down the street and right into the waiting arms of Officer Parsons, who'd lock me in the animal shelter.

Instead I raced around the outside of Mica's house half a dozen times until I was out of breath and collapsed on the front lawn. Foo-Foo collapsed beside me. Mica collapsed beside her. Andy collapsed beside Mica, and Josh collapsed beside Andy.

We all lay on the grass exhausted and gasping for breath.

Finally, Josh sat up. "What was that all about?"

"I forget," said Andy.

"It started with Foo-Foo chasing Lance," Mica explained.

"Right," Josh said and turned to Andy. "I hate to spoil the party, but we have to go *right now.* Understand?"

Andy glanced at Mica, then said to Josh, "Suppose I give you the key to my house and tell you where the comic is?"

Grrrrrrr . . . . In a flash I was on my feet, I mean, paws. I bared Lance's teeth and growled angrily at Andy.

"You can have the nose piece," Andy said to me.

"Why are you talking to Lance?" Mica asked.

"It's not gonna work, Andy," Josh said.

"What's not going to work?" Mica asked.

"Wait a minute," Andy said. "Where's Jake?"

Everyone looked around. Lance in my body had disappeared.

"Uh-oh." Josh pointed at Mica's front door.

It was wide open.

36

"I really wish someone would tell me what's going on," Mica said as Josh and Andy jumped to their feet and ran toward her front door.

"I will," Andy panted. "Soon . . . I promise."

I followed them.

Yap! Yap! Yap! Foo-Foo followed me.

From the front door of Mica's house we could see through the living room and into the kitchen.

The kitchen floor was covered with garbage. And lying in the middle of it was Lance in my body. Asleep, as usual.

"Oh, my gosh!" Mica gasped. "What a mess!"

"Don't worry," Andy said. "We'll clean it up."

"Not now we won't," Josh said, stepping into the kitchen and grabbing Lance in my body by the collar of the coveralls. "We've got someplace to go first."

"But we can't just leave Mica with this mess," Andy said.

"Wanna bet?" Josh yanked Lance in my body to

his feet. Lance blinked his eyes, looking both surprised and sleepy. He yawned.

"I wish someone would tell me what's going on," Mica said.

Ruff! Lance in my body stretched. Then he started scratching his ear. Mica stared at him in disbelief.

"To be honest, it's a long story," Josh said as he led Lance in my body away. "I'm sure Andy would love to explain it to you later. But right now we have to go."

"I can't leave Mica like this." Andy refused to budge.

Josh stopped. "Hey, Mica, did Andy ever tell you what he can do with a spitball? It's really amazing. You see, he — "

"Well, I guess it's time to go," Andy interrupted, and shoved Josh out of the kitchen.

I followed Andy.

Yap! Yap! Yap! Foo-Foo started to follow me.

Grrrrrr . . . I turned around and bared Lance's teeth at her.

Yiiiiiiii! She scampered away and straight into Mica's arms.

Andy waved sheepishly at Mica. "Well, er, it was really nice talking to you. I hope we can do it again sometime."

Mica stood in the middle of her kitchen with Foo-Foo in her arms. The floor around her feet was covered with garbage. She didn't look happy.

37

"You ruined everything!" Andy sputtered as we headed back toward school. "I mean, you totally messed things up between Mica and me!"

"I'm just making sure you keep your half of the deal," Josh replied.

"What would be so bad about Jake staying in Lance's body until tomorrow?" Andy asked.

"That's not the point," Josh replied. "The point is the comic book show is *tonight*. And so is the deadline for The Holey Donut Face Puzzle Contest. And a deal's a deal."

"But did you see Mica?" Andy asked. "She'll probably never speak to me again."

"Sure she will," Josh said. "Just don't bring Lance."

"Talk about Lance," Andy said as we hurried down the sidewalk toward school. "Just how do you plan to get him into school to make the switch? You know dogs aren't allowed."

"We're going to have to sneak in," Josh said.

"The conference is probably almost over. All those teachers will be in a rush to get home. We may get lucky."

We turned the last corner and headed toward school. Just as Josh had predicted, cars were pulling out of the parking lot.

"The conference must've just ended," Josh said.

Still holding the collar of Lance's, I mean, my coveralls, Josh led us to a side door near the science wing and pushed it open. We peeked in. The hall was empty.

"Okay," Josh whispered. "Let's go. Just be quiet."

We tiptoed into the hall. Mr. Dirksen's room was a few doors down, and we hurried toward it. We were just about to go in when the scent of shoe leather floated into my, I mean, Lance's nose.

A split second later, Principal Blanco turned the corner. "Hey, wait!" he shouted. "Stop!"

"Busted!" Andy mumbled under his breath.

38

Principal Blanco hurried toward us. Josh and Andy shared a miserable look. Not only were we busted, but we were busted bad. The list of things we'd done wrong was a long one.

We'd lied about being janitors-in-training and working for Dunstable Cleaning and Maintenance. We'd made him look like a fool in front of Ms. Governor's Commission on Excellence in Education. We'd come into school on a day when no students were allowed, *and* we'd brought a dog with us.

"Feels like suspension time," Josh muttered under his breath.

Principal Blanco reached us. He crossed his arms and stared at Lance in my body in the dark green coveralls. Then he looked down at me in Lance's body and frowned.

We braced ourselves.

Then Principal Blanco sighed.

He actually looked relieved. "Boy, am I glad to see you."

Josh, Andy, and I shared an amazed look. "Huh?"

39

Principal Blanco started back down the hall away from us. We stood in shock and watched him. Suddenly he must have realized we weren't following him. He turned and waved. "Come on, we don't have much time."

"Time for what?" Josh asked as we started to follow him.

"Time to find Ms. Stuart from the Governor's Commission," Principal Blanco replied and started to jog ahead.

"Do you have any idea what's going on?" Andy asked as we hurried after the principal.

"None," Josh replied, pulling Lance in my body. "I just know that whatever it is, we better play along."

Down the hall we saw Principal Blanco go into a room. A second later he came back out with Ms. Stuart. She looked as confused as we felt.

"They came back, Ms. Stuart," our principal said breathlessly. "I knew they would. You have

110

to understand about what happened this morning. It was just a joke. These three are the biggest practical jokers in school." Principal Blanco gave us a stern look. "Am I right, boys?"

We nodded. Ms. Governor's Commission stared down at me in Lance's body. "Is it my imagination, or is that dog nodding?"

"Uh, smart dog," Josh said.

"Now, boys," Principal Blanco said. "Once and for all, I want you to tell Ms. Stuart that you were only playing a joke this morning. You're not *really* custodians in training, are you?"

Josh and Andy shook their heads.

"Tell her what you really plan to do with your lives," he said.

"I plan to be a neurosurgeon," Josh said.

Principal Blanco nodded approvingly. "And what about you, Andy?"

"A game-show contestant," Andy said.

Principal Blanco and Ms. Stuart frowned.

"On College Bowl," Andy added.

Now they smiled. Ms. Governor's Commission turned to Lance in my body.

"And what about you, young man?" she asked.

Ruff! Lance in my body barked.

Ms. Stuart shrugged. "Well, I guess *someone* has to be a custodian."

"So you see?" Principal Blanco said eagerly. "It was a joke. I'm sure you'll want to note in your report that the *vast* majority of students here at

Burt Itchupt Middle School have great ambitions and high expectations for the future."

"Well, I certainly will reconsider," Ms. Stuart said. "Unfortunately I really do have to leave."

"Let me walk you to your car," Principal Blanco said. "On the way I'll tell you about some of our other students."

Principal Blanco started to walk Ms. Stuart toward the exit.

Josh quickly turned to the rest of us. "I think we just got a lucky break, guys. Now, come on!"

40

Once again we hurried to Mr. Dirksen's science lab. This time we made it inside without a problem.

Josh looked down at me in Lance's body. "Okay, Jake, you know what to do. Go over to the reclining chair and sit." Then he turned to Andy and told him to take Lance in my body over to the other chair. "When I give you the word, push him into the chair and step back."

Andy led Lance in my body over to the chair. Josh tapped the keys on the computer. "Okay, now!"

Andy pushed Lance into the chair.

Josh pushed the red button.

I shut my eyes.

Whump!

41

When I opened my eyes, I was back in my body.

Oowwooooo! In the other chair, Lance let out a howl and jumped down to the floor. He raced to the door of the science lab and scratched at it with his paw.

"There's one dog who knows what to do," Josh said, then turned to me. "You all right, Jake?"

I shook my head. I was in the process of feeling what it was like to be back in my own body, and I'd just gotten to my stomach. Queasy City!

"What's wrong?" Andy asked.

"What do you think is wrong?" Josh asked. "All he's had to eat today was garbage and dog food."

I tried to stand up, but I couldn't. I was bent over, holding my churning stomach.

"Think you can walk?" Josh asked.

"Do I have a choice?" I asked back.

"Actually, no." Josh went to the door and held it open. "Not unless you want to see Principal

Blanco again. And believe me, the next time we see him, he's not going to be so friendly."

I staggered to the door, holding my stomach. Meanwhile, Josh picked up Lance's leash so he couldn't get away when the door opened. A second later we all went out into the hall.

"That way!" Josh pointed to an exit at the far end of the hall. "We'll go around the back of the school. Principal Blanco won't see us."

42

Even with me holding my aching stomach and walking at a snail's pace, we actually made it home.

"Where have you been?" Jessica gasped when we came into the house. She rushed past me and kneeled in front of Lance. She threw her arms around his neck and hugged him. "I was so worried about you!" She looked up at us. "Is he okay?"

Josh, Andy, and I nodded.

"Jessica?" a voice asked. We looked up. A tall, handsome guy wearing a tight white T-shirt and jeans came out of the kitchen. He had big muscles and a chiselled, movie-star face.

Jessica smiled up at him. "Boys, this is Kirk. Kirk, this is my brother, Jake, and his friends Andy and Josh."

"Pleased to meet you." Kirk shook my hand. He squeezed so hard I thought it was going to break.

Jessica slipped her arm around Kirk's waist.

"Want to hear some great news? Kirk grew up with Labrador retrievers. He's had them all his life and he knows exactly how to train them so they don't go through the garbage."

"And nothing would make me happier than helping you, babe," Kirk said and gave my sister a quick peck on the cheek.

Jessica beamed.

"Hey, pup." Kirk reached down and rubbed Lance's head affectionately. "Let's go back into the kitchen and learn how to be a good dog."

Lance trotted down the hall toward the kitchen, and Kirk and Jessica followed, holding hands.

"Now I've seen everything," Andy moaned.

"No, you haven't," Josh said. "You haven't seen yourself giving me the fifth issue of Mole Man and Jake the nose piece. The comic book show opens in two hours."

"And the post office is open late tonight," I added. *Urp!* A little burp escaped from my lips. It smelled like dog food. I felt ill.

"Think you can make it to Andy's house?" Josh asked.

I nodded. I was determined to get the nose piece and send in the complete Holey Donut Face Puzzle by the midnight deadline.

"I bet Jake'll never be able to look at dog food again," Andy quipped as we headed to his house.

"Hey, it probably wasn't that bad," chuckled

Josh. "Remember what his sister said? *Canine Connoisseur* provides all the vital nutrients and vitamins you need."

"Oh, sure," I said with a groan. "Fish eyes . . . chicken noses . . . really great stuff."

"Yum." Andy licked his lips. "That stuff would be great on pizza."

I stared at him in disgust. "You are one sick puppy, Andy."

Andy and Josh shared a look and grinned.

"I think you've got it wrong, Jake," Josh said with a chuckle. "*You're* the sick puppy."

About the Author

Todd Strasser has written many award-winning novels for young and teenage readers. Among his best-known books are *Help! I'm Trapped in Obedience School* and *Girl Gives Birth to Own Prom Date*. He speaks frequently at schools about the craft of writing and conducts writing workshops for young people. He and his family live outside New York City with their yellow Labrador retriever, Mac. His latest project for Scholastic is a series about Camp Run-a-Muck, the grossest summer camp ever.